Thursday

After school we went to watch
Dad playing his fiddle
in the village band.

Friday

The Pinkpaws twins
have MORE new ballet
outfits. They're the biggest
showoffs in Mouseland!

Saturday

I spent ALL my pocket money in
Mrs Thimble's shop. But I
have to have new ribbons for
my ballet shoes, don't I?

Sunday

We all went to visit Grandma
and Grandpa for tea today.
Grandma makes the
best cheesecake!

This Angelina Ballerina Annual belongs to

Angelina™
Ballerina

ANNUAL 2004

Contents

You'll find a special Angelina Ballerina Annual competition at the end of the book. Make sure you enter – there are lots of super prizes for the winners!

Written by Brenda Apsley
Edited by Brenda Apsley and
Jane Clempner

Stories adapted from original scripts by
Mellie Buse, Paul Larson, Diane
Redmond and Barbara Slade

Designed by Sally Metcalfe

Based on the text by Katharine Holabird.
Illustrations by Helen Craig.

Angelina, Angelina Ballerina, and the
Dancing Angelina logo are trademarks of
HIT Entertainment PLC, Katharine
Holabird and Helen Craig Ltd. Angelina
is registered in the U.K. and Japan and
with the U.S. Patent and Trademark
Office. The Dancing Angelina logo is
registered in the U.K.

Published in Great Britain in 2003
by Egmont Books Limited,
239 Kensington High Street,
London W8 6SA.
Printed in Italy
ISBN 0 7498 5905 9

Meet ... Angelina Ballerina

**Turn the page to read all about Angelina
and her magical world ...**

All about Angelina

Angelina is a little white mouse with a wonderful dream. She wants to be a ballerina, a REAL ballerina. She loves to dance more than anything else in the world, and she's a natural dancer who just loves to be centre-stage. Angelina is determined to work hard at her ballet lessons to make her dreams come true. She knows it's not always going to be easy, but practice makes perfect.

"Dancing is absolutely the best thing ever!"

Angelina may be a little mouseling, but she has BIG ideas. She likes to get her own way, and she can be stubborn sometimes, but that's because she always wants to do her very best. When things don't go her way, Angelina gets frustrated and upset, but as soon as she hears the music and starts to dance, she's happy again.

Angelina loves fun and adventure, but her wild streak can get her into tight corners and trouble. Some of her adventures are funny, some are sad – and some are even a bit scary! But Angelina is clever and brave, and when she gets in a tight spot, she somehow manages to fix things in her own special way.

Angelina always tries to be good – well, almost always! – and she knows what's right and wrong. She's not always selfish, and she does think about others, and helps where she can. She really tries to keep her temper, even when things are difficult – and some days things are **very** difficult! But even when she's jealous or angry, Angelina finds a way to get over it – and keep on twirling.

Angelina just loves to dance and play!

Let's meet Angelina's family

Angelina and her family live in Mouseland, in a little village called Chipping Cheddar. It's a pretty place, with lots of houses and shops. There's a school and a village hall, too.

There are lots of little cottages in the village, and in one of them live Angelina and her family. Angelina's cottage is old, with lots of wooden beams and a roof made of thatch. There's a big kitchen, and a sitting room that's always warm and cosy, with a fire burning in the big fireplace.

Mr Maurice Mouseling is Angelina's dad. He owns the local newspaper, the Mouseland Gazette. He reports on all the village news.

"Dad's got his paw on what's happening around here!"

Mr Mouseling loves playing his fiddle at parties or with the village band. He likes jokes, and he's a lot of fun. But the thing he loves most of all is his family.

Mrs Matilda Mouseling

is Angelina's mum. She's the one Angelina
runs to when she's angry or upset, because
she's always ready with loving arms and a big
hug. Snuggling up on her lap makes Angelina's
troubles and problems melt away.

"The best mum in the world."

Mum always has just the right advice
for Angelina – though Angelina doesn't always
take it! She's patient, and hardly ever gets angry,
even when Angelina does her best to annoy her. Her voice is
kind, and her words are wise. But she's not soppy, and she can be
firm when Angelina REALLY misbehaves.

Mrs Mouseling loves cooking, and her Cheddar cheese pies are
famous. She's a good seamstress, and makes lovely ballet
costumes for Angelina. She likes doing odd jobs, too, like
mending leaky taps, and even building garden walls.

Polly is Angelina's baby sister. She's brown,
and as cute as a button. Angelina wasn't sure if
she really wanted a sister, but from the moment
Polly arrived Angelina loved her. She's turned
the family's world upside down – but Angelina
wouldn't have it any other way!

"Being a big sister is a whole lot of fun!"

Say hello to some very special mice

Grandma and Grandpa

are Angelina's grandparents. They live in the next village, so they often come to visit for a family party – or sometimes to take Angelina to the park or for a fancy cream tea.

Grandpa is old, and dark grey. He sometimes walks with a stick, but he's full of fun, and gives very wise advice, too. Angelina knows he's a real softie, with a heart of gold. He has a warm smile, and speaks in a gentle voice. He likes telling stories – and Angelina just loves listening to them.

"Grandpa's stories are brilliant!"

Grandma is pale grey, and wears little glasses on the end of her nose. Like Grandpa, she's an old softie, and she loves spoiling Angelina and her baby sister, Polly. She can seem a little gruff at times, but it's only because she likes good table manners.

"Grandma wants me to behave like a little lady."

Angelina has lots of friends and neighbours in Chipping Cheddar.

Mrs Hodgepodge lives next door. She's very old, and a bit bad tempered. She doesn't like noise, she doesn't like mouselings – and she doesn't like dancing! Angelina loves dancing anytime, anywhere, but Mrs Hodgepodge thinks that streets and gardens are NOT the place for it, and tells her so! Angelina tries to keep out of her way!

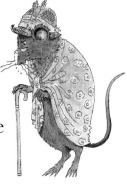

"Mrs Hodgepodge thinks dancing shouldn't be allowed - no prancing around in public!"

The only time Mrs Hodgepodge doesn't look grumpy is when she's in her garden. She's very proud of her flowers and vegetables, and keeps the mouselings as far away from them as possible!

Doctor Tuttle is the friendly village doctor. Angelina and her little sister visit him for their check-ups.

"Doctor Tuttle always gives us a cheesy mint when he measures our tails!"

Mrs Thimble runs the village shop. It sells just about everything, and Angelina and Alice often go there to spend their pocket money on fruits and sweets – and new ribbons for their ballet shoes, of course!

"It's such a treat to visit Mrs Thimble's shop."

Mr Bell is the old postman who always comes to Angelina's Christmas show in his Father Christmas costume. He loves to joke and tell stories to all the mouselings.

"Mr Bell always thinks my show is wonderful!"

Meet Angelina's friends

Alice Nimbletoes is Angelina's best friend. She's a little brown mouse with a heart of pure gold. She's happy and jolly, and she's the very best friend for someone like Angelina, because she helps her keep her paws on the ground.

Alice loves ballet, though she's not as good as Angelina. She loves dressing up in fancy costumes and twirling across the room, but she sometimes forgets her steps, and makes her stage entrances at the wrong time! She's a bit clumsy, too, so things can go wrong when she's around! But everyone loves Alice – especially Angelina. She's always there with a kind word, a happy smile, or a shoulder to cry on.

"I couldn't wish for a better best friend than Alice!"

Alice loves reading books, and knows about all sorts of odd things!

Alice laughs at silly things, and her giggles make everyone join in. Sometimes she laughs so much that she gets the hiccups!

Henry is Angelina's cousin. He's a very sweet little brown mouseling with long whiskers. People always say, "Oh, isn't he cute!" – which is not always what Angelina wants to hear! It can make her feel jealous sometimes.

"Henry can be a pest – but I love him, really!"

Henry loves his big cousin Angelina, and he likes to share her adventures. He gets very excited when he's allowed to take part in a ballet class with Angelina.

Henry is very up or very down. It's easy to see the mood he's in, because he bounces when he's happy, but if he's feeling sad, he looks very miserable.

Sammy Watts is Angelina's friend – well, most of the time! When he's cheeky and up to mischief, Angelina thinks he's very good fun. But when he teases Angelina and plays tricks on her, she's not so sure!

Sammy's a bit older than Angelina, and is often naughty. He's the one who gets the blame when bicycle tyre prints appear in Mrs Hodgepodge's flower beds. He sometimes tries to get the better of Angelina, but she usually finds a clever way to teach him a

"I'm more than a match for Sammy!"

Miss Lilly's ballet school

Miss Lilly is not just a friend to Angelina, she's her all-time hero and role model. She used to be a ballerina herself, so she has lived the life Angelina dreams of. Now that her dancing days are over, she wants to pass on her skills to youngsters like Angelina who want to follow in her pawsteps.

To Miss Lilly, life is dance, and dance is life. She lives and breathes it.

"As Miss Lilly says: 'Dance is everything'!"

Miss Lilly is from Dacovia, and she likes to be colourful. She wears big, bold jewellery and wraps her head in bright scarves. There's never a dull moment when she's around.

Angelina loves Miss Lilly. As far as Angelina is concerned, Miss Lilly is the cleverest and most beautiful dancer she's ever met. Angelina adores listening to Miss Lilly's stories about all the wonderful ballets and brilliant ballerinas she's known.

"Lift up your tails and dance!"

Angelina practises ballet every day because she wants to please Miss Lilly and be her star pupil. Miss Lilly loves all her students, but Angelina is her favourite. That's because Angelina reminds Miss Lilly of herself when she was a young ballet-mad mouseling.

William is one of Angelina's very best friends, and attends Miss Lilly's school. He likes ballet, but he's not a very good dancer. He's rather tall, and his long legs seem to get in the way.

"Miss Lilly chooses William to play parts like a palm tree!"

William is shy, and not very confident – unlike Angelina! When he's nervous he sometimes mixes up his words. This often happens when Angelina's near, because he has a bit of a crush on her!

Angelina has lots of friends at ballet school – but there are some pupils she's not so friendly with, like **Penelope and Priscilla**, the Pinkpaws twins. They are very spoiled, and always have the best dancing outfits money can buy, and all the latest toys.

"Those Pinkpaws twins can be very sneaky!"

The twins like to get their own way, and try to get the better of Angelina. They are good dancers, but they don't have Angelina's natural talent, and this makes them jealous. There's usually a battle going on between the twins and Angelina!

The Rose Fairy Princess

One day, the dancers at Miss Lilly's ballet studio were trying out for parts in a new show. Angelina was dancing well – as usual – but the Pinkpaws twins, Priscilla and Penelope, were trying to spoil her chances, and moved in front of her, so that she was hidden!

That made Angelina angry. "Those twins are too much!" she whispered to Alice.

"Don't worry," said Alice. "You'll get the part of the Rose Fairy Princess, I know you will!"

When Priscilla saw that the ribbon of Angelina's ballet slipper was undone, she was about to tell her. But Penelope put her paw over her sister's mouth, and smiled a sneaky smile.

As Angelina danced, the ribbon wrapped itself around her feet. When she tried to do her final leap, she fell to the floor with a bump.

"Never mind," said Penelope. "You can be in the chorus of dancing flowers!"

Miss Lilly told the pupils which parts they had. "The Rose Fairy Princess will be danced by ..."

Penelope jumped up and down. "Oh, I knew I'd get the part!" she said.

Miss Lilly looked surprised. "I am sorry, Penelope darlink.

Angelina will be the Rose Fairy Princess," she said. "But you will be a wonderful dancing flower!"

Later, Angelina and Alice heard Miss Lilly talking to the stage manager. "A perfect idea for the finale!" said Miss Lilly. "Yes, my Rose Fairy Princess will fly across the stage on a single wire!"

Angelina's eyes opened wide. "A single wire?" she said. "A SINGLE WIRE?"

Angelina went to see Miss Lilly. "I was just wondering if this single wire is a good idea," said Angelina. "I mean, the audience might see the wire and ... er ... it might, er ..."

Miss Lilly realised that Angelina was worried about 'flying' on a wire. She hugged her. "You are a funny little mouseling!" she said. "Don't worry. You will fly across the stage like ... a bird! You will be – magnificent!"

But Angelina still wasn't happy about the wire. "It's just one little thin wire!" she told Alice as they rode their bikes across the Village Green. "What if it snaps?"

"I'm sure it won't," said Alice.

But Angelina wasn't listening. She pedalled faster, leaving her friend behind. "Hurry, Alice!" she called. "We've got to find Zivo!"

Alice was puzzled. "Who's Zivo?"

But Angelina still wasn't listening. "Come on!"

Alice caught up with her friend outside a large circus tent. Angelina read out the words on a poster. "The Magnificent Zivo. The most daring circus trapeze artist. Yes!"

She grabbed Alice's hand and pulled her inside.

"Er, Mister Zivo, can you help me fly on a single wire?" called Angelina.

Zivo, who was hanging

from a trapeze by his little toe, did a triple flip, and landed beside her. "You have come to the right place, little mouseling," he said. "Come!"

Zivo made Angelina work hard.

First she jumped on the trampoline, higher and higher ...

Next she sailed backwards and forwards on the giant swing ...

Then she climbed to the top of the very tall ladder ... until at last, she was ready to fly.

She flew from trapeze to trapeze. One ... two ...

But at trapeze number three, Angelina saw a single wire ... and panicked! She lost her grip on the bar and fell, landing in the safety net.

"Ouch!" said Alice.

"Are you ready for the finale?" Miss Lilly asked at the next rehearsal.

Angelina stared at the wire. She couldn't move!

"Angelina?" said Miss Lilly.

Angelina put her hand on her forehead and weaved around as if she was dizzy. She winked at Alice, spun around ... and fell to the floor!

Priscilla saw the wink. "I think our Rose Fairy Princess is afraid of flying!" she whispered.

"Where am I?" said

Angelina. "I must have fainted ..."

"So she can't dance the part, can she?" said Penelope. "But I can, Miss Lilly. I know every step!"

"Angelina will be fine," said Miss Lilly. "Now don't worry, my darlink, no more flying today."

"What am I going to do, Alice?" said Angelina on the night of the ballet.

"I don't know," said Alice. "I'd fly for you if I could, but ..."

A big grin appeared on Angelina's face. "That's it!" she said. "Alice, **you** can fly across the stage instead of me. We'll change costumes. No one will ever know!"

Just before the finale, Angelina danced off one side of the stage, and Alice danced off the other. In the darkness at the back of the scenery, Angelina waited so they could change costumes. But Alice did not appear. "Where are you?" whispered Angelina.

Alice didn't hear her. Her costume was caught on a nail on the fairy castle, and she couldn't move!

When the music began, Angelina looked at Miss Lilly, and knew what she had to do. "I won't let you down, Miss Lilly," she said to herself. Then she strapped herself to the wire, took a big breath – and the Rose Fairy

Princess flew and soared and swooped across the stage!

The audience gasped, then jumped to their feet, and cheered and clapped.

As she flew across the stage, Angelina's expression turned from fear ... to wonder ... to excitement ... to pure joy. Flying was ... just wonderful!

Backstage, Alice gave a big pull, and her costume came free. But the pull made the fairy castle wobble. It shook ... then fell flat on to the floor of the stage. Penelope ended up sitting in the wreckage with a flower pot on her head!

A few days later, Angelina was still talking about flying. "I'm going to talk to Miss Lilly about a ballet about a circus girl," she told Alice. "She'll fly across the stage on a single wire! Played by me, of course!"

Angelina spun across the room, and Alice looked worried. "Angelina," she said. "I don't ..."

But Angelina wasn't listening. "It will be the best ballet ever!"

Angelina's ballet school puzzle

"A performance at Miss Lilly's ballet school is always an extra-special occasion. Look carefully – which of the things in the little pictures can you see in the big one? Write a tick for yes or a cross for no in each box."

"Friends are ..."

"I love my friends – they're really special. They make me glad sometimes – and they make me mad sometimes! But I still love them. And I know that they love me, which makes **me** feel really special, too."

"Friends are ... always pleased to see you."

"Friends are ... cuddly."

"Friends are ... clever.

"Friends are ... annoying!"

"Friends are ... kind."

"Are your friends special?
Write their names here.
Can you say a word that best
describes each of them?"

_____

_____

_____

_____

_____

_____

_____

_____

"Friends are ... sorry."

Angelina's Valentine

1 One morning, Angelina was busy at the kitchen table. "There!" she said, pushing a card into an envelope. "I've made Valentine cards for all my favourite people."

2 The biggest card was for Miss Lilly. Angelina read the message. "Roses are red, violets are blue. To you, dear Miss Lilly, my heart will be true."

3 William was busy, too. He was in Mrs Thimble's shop, choosing a Valentine card to send to Angelina. It had a big purple bow on the front.

4 Alice was in the shop, too. "Which chocolate heart will Henry like best?" she asked William. "The one with red icing, or the lilac one?"

William tried to hide the card, but he dropped it. Alice smiled. "Who is that pretty Valentine for?" she asked – but William wasn't saying!

Later, William stood outside Angelina's house with the card. It said, "Roses are red, violets are blue. Sugar is sweet – Angelina is too!"

Sammy was practising his double twizzler flick for the yo-yo competition. "Are you going to give that card to Angelina?" he asked.

William's eyes opened wide. "Give it to her?" he said. "No, I can't do that – she might see me!" Sammy shook his head, and walked off, spinning his yo-yo.

9. A noise that came from Angelina's garden made Sammy stop and look over the hedge. It was Angelina's new musical yo-yo. "Wow!" said Sammy.

10. Sammy had an idea. He hid his yo-yo, and went back to where William was still standing. "I'll deliver that Valentine for you ..." he said.

11. Sammy went into Angelina's garden and asked if he could try her new yo-yo, but she shook her head. "No, I'm busy practising."

12. "Oh, I see. You won't want this then, will you?" said Sammy, taking the card from behind his back, then showing it to Angelina.

13

"A Valentine!" said Angelina. She was very surprised. "Is it for me?" she asked. Sammy smiled. "Yes, why not?" he said. "Bye. See you later."

14

Sammy told William that he should buy something to go with the card, so they went to Mrs Thimble's shop, where William chose a red rose posy.

15

William was too shy to give the posy to Angelina, so he gave it to Sammy to give to her. "Oh, I hope she likes it!" said William.

16

Sammy smiled as he held out the posy. "A rose for a rose," he said sweetly. Angelina was VERY surprised. "For me?" she asked. "It's lovely. Thank you."

17

Sammy sighed. "I guess I'll just have to watch the yo-yo competition," he said. "Mine is broken, and it's too late to get another. Oh, well ..."

18

Angelina looked at the posy, then at her yo-yo. She ran after Sammy. "Here," she said, "you can borrow my yo-yo." Sammy was VERY pleased: "YA-HAY!"

19

Henry asked Angelina if she liked William's posy. "Yes," said Angelina. "But it's from Sammy, not William." Henry shook his head. "No, William sent it."

20

Alice looked thoughtful. "You know, I saw William buying a card just like the one Sammy gave you." Angelina stared. "I think I smell a RAT!"

21

Sammy was showing off his yo-yo tricks when Angelina said, "Sammy, will you say that sweet verse you wrote in my Valentine card for Alice?"

22

Sammy didn't know the words – but William did, and he said them out loud. Angelina took her yo-yo from Sammy and said, "I need this for the competition!"

23

Later that day, William got a card. The words inside made him smile. "Edam is red, Stilton is blue. Cheesecake is sweet – but not as sweet as you!"

24

"But who sent it?" said William. "Oh, could it be …?" Angelina knows who sent the card! Do you? You do? Well, don't tell William. It's a secret!

"I love ..."

"I love lots of people and lots of things. These are some of my special super-favourite things!"

"I love ... ribbons and bows."

"I love ... flowers."

"I love ... Mum and Dad."

"I love ... balloons."

"I love ... presents."

"I love ... Polly."

"I love ... Miss Lilly."

"I love ... my cousin, Henry."

"I love ... my best friend, Alice."

"Who and what do you love most? Why not write a list like mine, or make a poster, with names and pictures?"

"Sometimes I feel ..."

"sometimes I feel glad, sometimes I feel sad – and sometimes I just feel so mad, mad, MAD!"

"sometimes I feel ... excited!"

"sometimes I feel ... angry!"

"sometimes I feel ... sad."

"sometimes I feel ... MAD!"

"sometimes I feel ...
pleased with myself."

"sometimes I feel ...
poorly. Poor me!"

glad me

sad me

"What things make you glad or sad? Draw pictures of how you look when you're feeling happy or unhappy."

37

Angelina in the wings

Miss Lilly had some exciting news for Angelina and the other dancers. She pointed to a

poster on the wall. "The famous Madame Zizi is dancing in The Sun Queen, and she is coming here with Mr Popoff, the director, to take a class with YOU! One of the little sunbeam dancers in the ballet has the mouse pox, so she can't dance!"

Angelina leapt up. "Does that mean they want a

replacement?" she asked.

"Indeed it does!" said Miss Lilly.

Angelina could hardly wait to tell her parents. Neither could Henry. "Angelina's going to be a sunbeam!" he called, skipping around with his clockwork ladybug toy.

"But the Pinkpaws twins have got the costumes, Mum!" said Angelina.

Mrs Mouseling patted her paw. "It's not costumes that matter," she said.

"That's right," said Mr Mouseling. "And you'll have Henry there, for luck."

"WHAT?" said Angelina. "I have to take HENRY with me? Last time he came to class he spilled his drink and Priscilla slipped in it!"

Mr Mouseling laughed. "Henry doesn't have accidents like that anymore," he said – at the same moment as Henry's ladybug toy ran into his drink and spilled it all over the table!

The next day, Miss Lilly had more news for the mouselings. "Priscilla and Penelope have the mouse pox," she said, "so they cannot be here."

That was great news for Angelina. "Oh, hurr– !" she said, then stopped. "Er, that's bad news."

She turned and whispered to Alice. "Now this sunbeam is going to shine!"

Mr Popoff told the mouselings what he wanted them to do. "Skip! Run, and turn. Skip, skip! Run and turn. Yes, excellent!"

Madame Zizi was watching. "Charming!" she

said. Then she pointed to Angelina. "That leetle peenk mouseling!"

"Dance on your own please," said Mr Popoff.

All eyes were on Angelina as she danced across the room. Everyone was watching her – everyone except Henry. He was trying to keep still, but a fly was buzzing around his head, and when it landed on his nose, he flicked it off. But that made him drop his ladybug toy, and it set off across the studio floor.

Henry followed, but he couldn't catch it.

The ladybug scattered Alice and the other mouselings … then it made Angelina fall over as she was taking her bow … and came to a stop resting against Madame Zizi's feet!

It was very quiet, and everyone was watching as Henry picked up his toy.

But Madame Zizi wasn't angry. She picked Henry up and stood him on her chair. "Thees ees the sweetest leetle

mouseling!" she said. "We must have heem for the sunbeam! I insist!"

Then she pointed to Angelina. "And the peenk one will be his understudy, yes?"

Angelina didn't cry then, but she did when she was back in her bedroom with Alice. "I've got to watch – SOB! – while Henry gets to – SOB! – dance!" said Angelina. "Oh, Alice ..."

Alice tried to cheer her up. "Look, Madame Zizi will see how good you are, and add another sunbeam, especially if you add some twirls and ... oh, you know, fancy stuff!"

Angelina stopped crying as quickly as she had started. "Alice," she said, "you're a GENIUS!"

Angelina planned to get herself noticed. She jumped higher and better than all the other sunbeams, and Mr Popoff was very pleased with her.

But he was less pleased with Henry. He didn't jump when the others did, and he bumped into them. He seemed to have two left feet! "The boy mouseling can do nothing!" he said.

"But the audience weel LOVE heem!" said Madame Zizi.

Angelina's plan had not worked. But she had another idea. This time she would do lots of little jobs for Madame Zizi.

She was on her way to the wardrobe room when she bumped into Henry, who was lost.

"Where's the stage?" he asked.

"Not now, Henry!" said Angelina. "Can't you see I'm busy?"

The mouselings were already dancing when Henry arrived. He was very late.

"Eet ees not hees fault!" said Madame Zizi, lifting him in her arms. "Angeline did not look after heem as I told her to!"

Later, Angelina and Alice were at the side of the stage when they overheard Mr Popoff talking to Madame Zizi. "We have to use the understudy sunbeam," said Mr Popoff.

Angelina smiled. "That's ME!" she whispered.

"The boy mouseling has to go!" said Mr Popoff.

When she heard those words, the smile left Angelina's

face. She wanted to be a sunbeam, but she didn't want to take Henry's place! She ran on to the stage. "Please give him a chance. I'll help him! Pleeeeease!"

"Yes," said Madame Zizi. "He weel have one more chance. I inseest!"

Angelina worked hard with Henry. "You're going to be a great sunbeam!" she told him, and he was, because when another mouseling got mouse pox, Henry and Angelina BOTH danced.

"Perfect, Henry," said Mr Popoff. "Thanks to you, Angelina."

The next morning, Mrs Mouseling went into Angelina's bedroom with some cheesy niblets. "Alice sent them," she said, then she stopped and stared.

Sitting up in bed were Angelina and Henry – and they were both covered in big red spots. "Oh dear," said Mrs Mouseling. "Two little spotty sunbeams!"

Same ...
but different

"These two pictures of my bedroom look the same, but there are five things that are different in picture 2. Can you help me spot them all?"

1

2

"Here's another spot the differences puzzle for you.
I can find three things that are different in picture
2, but I know there are five differences to find. HELP!"

1

2

"It's fun to ..."

"I work hard because I know that's how to become a great ballerina like Miss Lilly. But I like to have fun, too! Here are some of the things I think are the BEST fun!"

"It's fun to ... dress up."

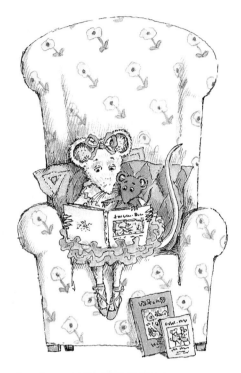

"It's fun to ... read to my baby sister, Polly."

"It's fun to ... help Dad in the kitchen."

"It's fun to ... watch Alice
doing hand stands!"

"It's fun to ... dance
with Henry."

"What fun things do you like? Write words if you
can, or ask a grown-up to help you."

It's fun to ...

It's fun to ...

It's fun to ...

47

1 One day, Mr Mouseling was in the garden, talking to Mrs Hodgepodge about the giant cauliflower she had grown. She was very proud of it.

2 Angelina and Alice were trying to put up a tent, so that they could camp out that night, but they weren't doing very well. It kept falling down!

3 Just then, a bicycle bell rang, and Sammy rode through a gap in the fence. He rode round the cauliflower and Mrs Hodgepodge – and out into the lane.

4 Mrs Hodgepodge chased after him, but he was too fast for her. "How many times do I have to tell you, Sammy Watts!" she cried. "This is NOT a shortcut!"

5   Angelina was hammering in the last tent peg when Sammy came back. "Bet you don't stay out all night," said Sammy. "Bet we do!" said Angelina.

6   "Bet you a jar of cheesy mints you don't!" said Sammy. "You'll run inside when the ghost of Old Red Whiskers comes to get you, I know you will!"

7   Alice looked worried. "Old Red Whiskers?" she asked. "Take no notice, Alice," said Angelina. "He's just trying to scare us. I'll tell you the story tonight."

8   That night, Angelina told Alice the story. "Just as Old Red Whiskers thought he was safe, along came a big tabby cat – and snapped off his tail!"

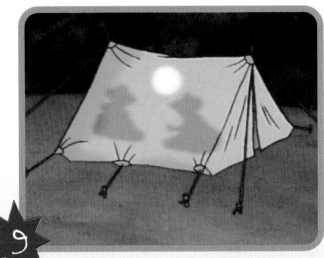

9 "Ever since that night, the ghost of Old Red Whiskers roams the garden, in search of fresh cheese," said Angelina. "And his missing tail!"

10 Just then, they heard a sound outside: **Wwwoooo!** Alice pulled her sleeping bag up around her ears. "Is it the ghost of Old Red Whiskers?"

11 They heard the noise again: **Wwwwwwooooooo!** "I don't know what it is," said Angelina. "But I'm going to find out." Alice jumped up. "Wait for me!"

12 It was VERY dark outside! Angelina looked around the shed. "Nothing there!" she said – just as Alice pointed to a long shadow in front of them!

13 Angelina moved the lantern along the shadow, then smiled. "It's just Dad's garden fork with his hat on the handle," she said. "You scaredy mouse, Alice!"

14 **Wwwwwoooooo!** When they heard the noise again, Angelina said, "It's coming from Mrs Hodgepodge's garden! Wait here, Alice!"

15 Angelina heard the noise again. She walked into a big, white sheet, which wrapped itself around her head, and she ran off in a panic! "Help ... leave me alone ..."

16 Angelina tripped, the sheet came off, and she ran off again. "Arrrggh!" she screamed, and bumped into ... Alice! Seconds later, they were in the house!

17 Next morning, Angelina found a little bit of Mrs Hodgepodge's cauliflower on her nightie. Angelina looked outside. "I must have trodden on it last night!" she said.

18 Later on, when Mrs Hodgepodge found Sammy in her garden, she blamed him for spoiling her cauliflower. "You little monster!" she cried.

19 Angelina and Alice baked a cake. They put it outside Mrs Hodgepodge's door with a little card that said 'I am really sorry. From Sammy'.

20 But Mrs Hodgepodge didn't see the cake. She stepped in it, slipped, and landed, SPLAT! The cake hit a garden gnome, and it broke into tiny pieces!

21 When Mrs Hodgepodge took Sammy's bike and put it up for sale to pay for a new gnome, Angelina knew that it was time for her to own up ...

22 She told Mrs Hodgepodge what had happened, and how sorry she was. Sammy was pleased that he wasn't being blamed.

23 "But you still owe me some cheesy mints!" said Sammy. "How do you know we didn't stay out all night?" asked Angelina.

24 "**Wooooooo!**" said Sammy, and Angelina's eyes opened wide. "So it was you!" she said, smiling. "You were the ghost of Old Red Whiskers!"

Mrs Thimble's shop

"I just love visiting Mrs Thimble's shop. So does Alice! We spend our pocket money there, because she sells more kinds of sweets than you could ever eat!"

Which of these things can you see in the big picture?
Point, say yes or no, then put a tick or a cross in each box.

Now count the numbers of things on these pages,
and write a number in each box.

55

"I like ..."

"*I always like to be on the go, dancing, performing, and having adventures with my friends.*"

"*I like ... dancing.*"

"*I like ... skating.*"

"*I like ... riding my bicycle.*"

56

"I like ... doing cartwheels with Alice."

"I like ... flying through the air!"

"I like ... running rings round little mouselings!"

"What things do **you** like doing? Are some of them the same as the things I like?"

57

The gift

It was Christmas, and the whole of Chipping Cheddar was under a soft white blanket of snow.

On the day of Miss Lilly's ballet studio party, the mouselings were busy, all except one ...

Angelina was looking at a little glass snow dome. When she shook it, tiny snowflakes swirled and whirled, then settled around a miniature ballerina wearing a pale green tutu.

"Isn't it lovely?" said Miss Lilly. "My very first ballet teacher gave it to me a long time ago. I was younger than you are now." She laughed. "Why, I could barely point my toes!"

"You mean you couldn't always dance?" asked Angelina.

"Of course not, darlink!" said Miss Lilly.

Just then there was a loud crash as Mr Mouseling and Doctor Tuttle started to push a very large Christmas tree into the room. Mr Mouseling was outside. "All clear?" he called.

Doctor Tuttle was inside. "Oh dear ..." he said.

"Right then!" said Mr Mouseling, and he pushed the tree so hard that it slid into the middle of the room.

Mr Mouseling came in. The mouselings were giggling, and there were pine needles everywhere. "Er, did you say 'all clear' or 'oh dear'?" he asked.

"I can't wait to see the tree with all our gifts on it," said Alice.

"Yes, I spent all week making my gift for Miss Lilly," said Angelina.

"How sweet!" said Penelope Pinkpaws. "A home-made gift."

"And we only got her an expensive necklace," said Priscilla. "Oh dear!"

Angelina emptied her piggy bank and went into the village with Alice and William. "I'm going to buy the perfect present for Miss Lilly," she told them.

She soon found what she was looking for. It was a big hat with feathers and ribbons and jewels on the front.

"That will be sixty-four pounds and ninety-nine pence," said the lady in the shop.

Angelina gulped. "Sixty-four ninety-nine!" she said. "I don't have enough money."

When Angelina, Alice and William passed some buskers playing music on the Village

When Angelina got home, she didn't look very happy.

"Why the long face?" asked Mrs Mouseling.

"It's my gift for Miss Lilly," said Angelina. "It's ..."

"... just perfect!" said Mrs Mouseling, holding out the picture Angelina had painted. "Look, I put it in a frame."

"But it's so ... HOME-MADE!" said Angelina, unhappily.

Green, they stopped to listen. At the end of their song, one of the buskers collected money from the audience.

"Alice, I've got an idea!" said Angelina, and soon there was more music on the Village Green. It was ballet music – and Angelina was dancing to it.

People stopped to watch, and at the end they gave William lots of money.

The friends raced back to the shop – but the hat had been sold!

"Oh, no!" said Angelina.

When it was time for the party, Mrs Mouseling found Angelina hiding under the bed. She wiped a tear from her cheek. "I'm not going to the party without a gift for Miss Lilly ..." she said sadly.

"But you have a gift for her," said Mrs Mouseling. "A very special gift. And Miss Lilly will be so upset if you don't go, won't she?"

Angelina nodded. "Yes. All right then, but …"

The mouselings sat around the Christmas tree as Miss Lilly opened her gifts. There was one on every branch, but Angelina had hidden hers round the back.

The last one was from Penelope and Priscilla. "What a lovely necklace!" said Miss Lilly. "Thank you, darlinks! And now

we will …"

"But there's one more gift," said Priscilla, crawling to the back of the tree. "It must be from Angelina!"

Angelina looked at her feet as Miss Lilly looked at the painting.

"Oh, it is SO beautiful!" she said.

"It is?" asked Angelina.

"Oh, yes," said Miss Lilly. "I love it, my darlink!"

"You do?" asked Angelina.

"I do," said Miss Lilly. "And I will put it here, on the wall."

Miss Lilly gave Angelina a big hug. "Thank you, little ballerina," she whispered. "A home-made gift comes right from the heart."

Angelina was telling Alice and William what she was going to make for Miss Lilly next year, when Mrs Hodgepodge arrived wearing the hat Angelina had wanted to buy! It looked rather silly, and everyone stared.

"Just look at that hat!" whispered Miss Lilly. "What a ... creation!"

Angelina looked at William, William looked at Alice, and Alice looked at Angelina. Then they all burst out laughing.

That night, Angelina opened her gift from Miss Lilly. It was the snow dome, with the little ballerina inside it! She shook it gently, and hundreds of tiny snowflakes swirled and twinkled.

Angelina was thrilled. "It's the very best gift in the world!"

Picture puzzles

Look carefully at the pictures of Angelina on this page.
Which two are just the same?

More pictures of Angelina! Which is the odd one out?

What do you know about Angelina?

Can you answer these questions about Angelina? Check your answers at the bottom of page 67.

1 Who lives next door to Angelina?

2 Alice Nimbletoes is Angelina's best friend. True or false?

3 What is Sammy's last name?

4 Which musical instrument does Angelina's dad play?

5 Which country does Miss Lilly come from? Is it Dacovia or Russia?

6 Angelina lives in a village called Cheesy Cheddar. True or false?

7 What are the names of the Pinkpaws twins?

8 How many brothers and sisters does Angelina have?

9 In the story called 'Angelina's Valentine' on page 28, who sent Angelina a Valentine card?

10 Who is the owner of the village shop?

11 Angelina's mum and dad are called Mary and Martin. True or false?

12 In the story called 'The gift' on page 58, what gift did Miss Lilly give Angelina?

Answers
1 Mrs Hodgepodge, 2 True, 3 Watts, 4 Fiddle, 5 Dacovia, 6 False – she lives in Chipping Cheddar, 7 Penelope and Priscilla, 8 She has one sister, called Polly, and no brothers, 9 William, 10 Mrs Thimble, 11 False – their names are Matilda and Maurice, 12 A snow dome with a ballerina inside it.

Angelina dreams of ...

Angelina dreams of... a beautiful pink costume.

Angelina dreams of ... Christmas.

Angelina dreams of ... being in the spotlight.

Angelina dreams of ... a magic wand, to make her dreams come true!

"What do you dream of? Draw a picture."

Angelina Competition Time

We have lots of fabulous Angelina prizes to give away in this easy to enter competition.

1st The **First Prize** winner will win this beautiful Angelina **Theatre Playset**, courtesy of Flair Leisure Products.

The set folds down into a portable storage case and features working curtain, stage lights, pivoting platform, Angelina swing and reversible scenery. The set also includes two collectable figures.

2nd

The **Second Prize** winner will win this 12" tall Angelina Prima Ballerina plush toy, again courtesy of Flair. It's every little girl's dream …

Flair Flair Leisure Products
Customer Services
Tel. no. 0208 643 0320